Irma Rangel

Published in the United States of America by Cherry Lake Publishing
Ann Arbor, Michigan
www.cherrylakepublishing.com

Content Adviser: Jessica Criales, Doctoral Candidate, History Department, Rutgers University
Reading Adviser: Marla Conn MS, Ed., Literacy specialist, Read-Ability, Inc.
Book Design: Jennifer Wahi
Illustrator: Jeff Bane

Photo Credits: ©Cartarium/Shutterstock, 5; ©cheapbooks/Shutterstock, 7; ©Belenos/Shutterstock, 9, 22; ©Texas House of Representatives, 11; ©amadeustx/Shutterstock, 13; ©Brandon Seidel/Shutterstock, 15, 23; ©PD Ccchhhrrriiisss, 17; ©Monkey Business Images/Shutterstock, 19; ©Texas House of Representatives, 21; Cover, 8, 12, 14, Jeff Bane; Various frames throughout, ©Shutterstock Images

Library of Congress Cataloging-in-Publication Data has been filed and is available at catalog.loc.gov

Printed in the United States of America
Corporate Graphics

About the author: Katie Marsico is the author of more than 200 reference books for children and young adults. She lives with her husband and six children near Chicago, Illinois.

About the illustrator: Jeff Bane and his two business partners own a studio along the American River in Folsom, California, home of the 1849 Gold Rush. When Jeff's not sketching or illustrating for clients, he's either swimming or kayaking in the river to relax.

my story

I was born in Texas. My family was Mexican American.

People from Spanish-speaking countries are called Hispanic.

4

I learned about **racism** early. Some white people didn't like us.

They didn't want Hispanic neighbors. But I wouldn't let racism get in my way.

How do you treat your neighbors?

I studied hard. I worked as a teacher.

Later, I became a **lawyer**.

There weren't many lawyers like me.

I was a woman. I was Hispanic.

What makes you special?

I didn't stop there.

Next, I became a **lawmaker**.

What are some laws
you would make?

I served in the state **legislature**.

I was the first Hispanic woman to do so.

I wanted everyone to be treated fairly. I worked hard for the poor.

I fought racism. All people should have the right to do the same things.

I believed there should be **equality** in school. I said state **colleges** should always accept certain students.

These students didn't have to be white. They just had to be the best in their class.

I died in 2003. But my efforts broke records.

My work changed lives.

What would you like to ask me?

1969

1930

↑
Born
1931

1976

2030

Died
2003

glossary

colleges (KAH-lij-iz) schools where students can continue to study after they have finished high school

equality (ih-KWAH-lih-tee) the right of everyone to be treated the same

lawyer (LAW-yur) a person who has studied the law and is trained to help people in this matter

lawmaker (LAW-may-kur) someone who is voted into office to help make laws

legislature (LEJ-is-lay-chur) a group of people who have the power to make or change laws for a country or state

racism (RAY-sih-zuhm) the belief that people who share certain physical traits (such as skin color) are better than those who don't

index